·OF·SWORDS· ·AND·SORCERERS·

OF SWORDS AND SORCERERS

THE ADVENTURES OF KING ARTHUR AND HIS KNIGHTS

BY MARGARET HODGES AND MARGERY EVERNDEN

WOODCUTS BY DAVID FRAMPTON

CHARLES SCRIBNER'S SONS · NEW YORK   MAXWELL MACMILLAN CANADA · TORONTO

MAXWELL MACMILLAN INTERNATIONAL · NEW YORK   OXFORD   SINGAPORE   SYDNEY

Charles Scribner's Sons Books for Young Readers
Macmillan Publishing Company
866 Third Avenue, New York, NY 10022

Maxwell Macmillan Canada, Inc.
1200 Eglinton Avenue East, Suite 200
Don Mills, Ontario M3C 3N1

Macmillan Publishing Company is part of the
Maxwell Communication Group of Companies.

First edition   10 9 8 7 6 5 4 3 2 1
Printed in the United States of America

Library of Congress Cataloging-in-Publication Data
Hodges, Margaret.
Of swords and sorcerers : the adventures of King Arthur and
his knights / Margaret Hodges and Margery Evernden.   p.   cm.
Summary: Nine episodes in the Arthurian cycle, from the placing of
the boy Arthur in Merlin's care to Arthur's departure for Avalon.
ISBN 0-684-19437-6
1. Arthurian romances.   [1. Arthur, King.   2. Folklore—England.
3. Knights and knighthood—Folklore.]   I. Evernden, Margery.   II. Title.
PZ8.1.H690f 1992 809'.93351—dc20 [398.2] 91-40811

TO

THE MEMORY OF

CECILE COX OFFILL,
storyteller *par excellence*,

AND

TO

SUZANNE OFFILL WOLFE,
devoted children's librarian

Foreword

For hundreds of years men and women, boys and girls, have listened to tales of King Arthur of Britain and the knights and ladies of his court. Tellers of these stories have shaped them according to their own vision, while relying heavily upon legends from the past. We ourselves owe a special debt to Sir Thomas Malory's *Le Morte d'Arthur*; to the Welsh collection of tales, the *Mabinogion*; and to the work of the American Howard Pyle.

In 1952 we two had the honor to be chosen as storytellers for a cycle of Arthurian legends at the Boys and Girls Room in the Carnegie Library of Pittsburgh. The third teller was Cecile Cox Offill, widely acclaimed for her thrilling renditions of ancient epics. Almost forty years later Mrs. Offill's daughter, Suzanne Offill Wolfe, brought us the manuscripts on which we had worked with her mother. This set us to work again, adding to the number of stories and blending our various styles of telling into a unified whole.

MARGARET HODGES

MARGERY EVERNDEN

Contents

·OF·SWORDS·
·AND·SORCERERS·

ONE

Of Castles and Dragons

In the ancient days of Britain there lived a king named Vorti-gern. He invited Saxon armies from across the seas to come to help him in his wars with rival kings. But the Saxons betrayed Vortigern and drove him into the mountains of Wales. There the king's wise men advised him to build a fortress which would withstand any attack.

Vortigern was pleased with this advice. He traveled with his wise men from one rugged mountain to another, searching for the best place to build his castle. At last they came to a lofty peak, which is now called Snowdon. This mountain commanded all the country round about, and the wise men said, "Build your fortress here. This place is surely safe from attack."

The king sent for stonemasons, carpenters, and craftsmen. They quarried stone and hewed down great trees. But when they began to build the castle, all their work seemed hopeless. Whatever they raised by day fell down in the night, and the stones and timber disappeared. Again and again the king's work-men tried to build the castle, but each morning their work was gone without a trace.

Vortigern called a council of his wise men and asked them to explain the mystery. They consulted the powers of earth and sky, and at last they answered the king, "Your citadel cannot be built without a blood sacrifice. First you must find a boy born without a father. Kill him and sprinkle his blood on the ground where you wish to build."

The king thanked his wise men for their advice and sent messengers to search for a boy who had been born without a father. For a long while they searched in vain.

But at last one day the messengers came to a field where several boys were playing ball. One of the boys, a lad with strange bright eyes and long dark hair, threw the ball and called out, "None of you can catch this." And although it looked like an easy throw, not one of the others caught it.

Again and again he threw. The ball seemed to curve in midair so that no one could catch it. Then the other boys began to taunt the thrower. "You never play fairly, you trickster, you boy without a father."

When the messengers heard this, they knew that they had found the boy they wanted. They seized him and took him to King Vortigern.

"Who is your father?" asked the king.

"I do not know," the boy answered.

Then the king sent for the mother and demanded to know who was the boy's father.

"I do not know," she said. "No man has ever been my lover.

But one night a noble and godlike personage came to me in a dream, and afterward this wonderful boy was born. Whether it was an angel or a beautiful devil who visited me, I do not know. But I am sure that this boy's father was no ordinary mortal. I have called my child Merlin the Magician."

King Vortigern sent the mother away and kept Merlin with him. The next day he assembled his wise men, his soldiers, and all his builders to witness the sacrifice of the boy's life at the place where the castle was to be built.

"Why have you brought me here?" asked Merlin.

"To put you to death," answered Vortigern. "Unless the ground is sprinkled with your blood, my castle will not stand."

The eyes of Merlin grew dark. "Who told you this?" he asked.

"My wise men," said the king.

"Let me question them," said Merlin. And when the wise men came forward, he said, "If you know that the king's castle will not stand unless my blood is sprinkled on the ground, you must know all things. Tell the king what is hidden under this ground."

But the wise men said, "We do not know."

Merlin said, "There is a pool under this place. Dig and you will find it."

The builders dug and found the pool, as Merlin had said.

"Now tell what is at the bottom of the pool," he commanded the wise men.

But they were confused, and said, "How can we know that?"

Merlin said to the king, "Your wise men do not know, but I do. Search the bottom of the pool and you will find two jars joined together."

The pool was searched, and the jars were found. "Now," said

Merlin, "if your wise men are truly wise, they can tell you what is in the jars."

Again the wise men did not know. "Break the jars," Merlin commanded, "and you will find a tent."

When the jars were broken, a folded tent appeared. "And what is within the folds of the tent?" Merlin asked the wise men. With shame, they confessed their ignorance.

"There are two dragons within," said Merlin. "Unfold the tent." And when the tent was unfolded, two sleeping dragons were seen, one blood red, with sun-colored wings, and one white, with talons of bright silver.

"Watch what they do," said Merlin.

The dragons then raised themselves and began to struggle with each other. And all the battles of all the years of the world were like quiet sleep compared with that battle of the two dragons. They flew upward and the valleys echoed with the beating of their wings. Their glorious scales flashed against the sky. Their fiery breath wounded the wind. The lashing of their forked tails cleft mountains asunder so that torrents and waterfalls poured out. On Mount Snowdon, Vortigern's men were almost blinded by the beauty and splendor of the dragons. And as their fighting grew more fierce and furious, the two dragons grew even stronger and more beautiful, their wings flaming up to heaven, then descending to earth in a halo of golden light. The white dragon drove the red dragon to the western edge of the tent. Then the red one, recovering his strength, fought ever more fiercely until he drove the white dragon eastward, and both disappeared.

"What is the meaning of this omen?" Merlin asked the wise

men. And when they again confessed that they did not know, he said to the king, "I will tell you. The pool is the symbol of the world, and the tent means your kingdom of Britain. The red dragon is the emblem of your people, and the white dragon is that of the Saxons. Even now they hold most of Britain, for the white dragon is stronger than the red one. But the red dragon will forever protect these western mountains. As for you, King Vortigern, depart from Snowdon. I foresee that you are not meant to build a fortress here."

Then King Vortigern dismissed his foolish wise men and spared Merlin's life.

In time, a hero named Uther took Vortigern's place as king of Britain, bearing as his emblem a silken banner emblazoned with the red dragon, so that he was called Uther Pendragon. Like Vortigern before him he fought valiantly to subdue and unite all the warring kings of Britain, but this he could never do.

Now Merlin had grown to manhood and become a very great magician. When he saw that the struggle for the kingdom would be longer than the life of Uther Pendragon, he found for him a wife, the fair Igraine. She was a young widow whose husband had been slain by Uther in battle, and she had her castle at Tintagel on the coast of Cornwall. There Uther wooed her, and there at Tintagel Arthur, son of Uther Pendragon, was born.

Soon after the birth, Merlin came to Uther and said, "Sir, I foresee that you have not long to live. You must give your son to me. Until he is grown to manhood I will keep him in hiding, safe from your enemies, who would kill him if they could. Bring him to me tonight at the postern gate of this castle."

Under cover of darkness, as Merlin commanded, the child was brought to him, wrapped in rich cloth of gold. Then Merlin carried him away and gave him into the care of a worthy knight, Sir Ector. This good man did not know that the child was the son of Uther Pendragon, but he loved Arthur like a father, and Sir Ector's wife nursed the baby as if he had been her own child.

Within two years, Uther Pendragon won a great victory over his enemies, but as Merlin had foretold, the king soon fell sick unto death. Then Merlin said to him, "Call your closest counselors together."

When this was done, Merlin stood before them and called aloud to King Uther so that all present could hear, "Sir, shall your son Arthur be king after you?"

And Uther said, "I give him God's blessing and mine, and I bid him to claim the crown." With these words the king died, but his counselors, swollen with their own ambitions, repeated nothing of what they had heard.

Now Arthur grew to be a man in the household of Sir Ector. He knew no other father, and he loved Sir Ector's son, Kay, like a brother. During these years the kingdom was in danger, for in spite of the king's last words, every lord and baron wished to seize the throne. At last, when the time was ripe, Merlin called all of them to London and told them that God would work a miracle to show who should be king. A throng of great men came to London and went into church to pray, for it was Christmastide.

When they came out again, they saw in the churchyard a great square stone. On the stone stood an anvil of steel a foot high, and thrust into the anvil they saw the blade of a fine sword, inscribed with letters of gold: WHOSO PULLETH OUT THIS SWORD OF THIS STONE AND ANVIL IS RIGHTWISE KING BORN OF ALL ENGLAND.

Then some of the lords, who wanted to be king, tried to pull the sword from the stone, but none could move it. While they were still waiting for the sign from God which Merlin had promised, New Year's Day came, and it was decided to hold a tournament.

Now Kay, Arthur's foster brother, had been newly knighted. Being small in stature, he longed to prove his valor in the tournament. But when he came to the field where the lists had been set up, he found that he had forgotten his sword. He asked Arthur to ride back to his father's lodging and bring his sword to him. Arthur rode back with a good will, and as he passed the churchyard, he saw the sword in the stone. When he came to Sir Ector's house, the door was locked, for all had gone to the jousting. Then Arthur said to himself, "I will ride to the churchyard and take that sword from the stone, for my brother, Kay, must have a sword."

When he came to the churchyard, he dismounted and tied his horse to the stile. He took the sword by the hilt, and lightly pulled it out of the stone. Then he rode back to Sir Kay and gave him the sword. As soon as Kay saw it, he knew that it was the sword of the stone, and he rode with it to his father and said, "Sir, here is the sword of the stone. Therefore I must be king of this land."

But when Sir Ector saw the sword, he made Arthur and Kay return with him to the church, and he made Kay swear an oath to tell truly how he came by the sword. "Sir," said Kay, "I got it from my brother, Arthur, who brought it to me."

"How did you get this sword?" Sir Ector said to Arthur.

"Sir, I will tell you," said Arthur. "When I went home for my brother's sword, I found the door locked and nobody there. So I came here and pulled the sword out of the stone."

"Did any knight see you do this?" asked Sir Ector.

"No," said Arthur.

Then Sir Ector said to Arthur, "None can be king but he who draws this sword. Let me see whether you can put the sword as it was and pull it out again."

"That is not difficult," said Arthur, and he put the sword into the stone again.

Then Sir Ector tried to pull out the sword and failed. Kay pulled at the sword with all his might, but it would not move.

"Now you shall try again," Sir Ector said to Arthur.

"I will," said Arthur, and pulled it out easily. Then Sir Ector and Sir Kay knelt before him.

"Alas," said Arthur, "my own dear father and brother, why do you kneel to me?"

"I never was your father, my lord Arthur," said Sir Ector. "Now I know that you are of nobler blood than I." Then he told Arthur how he had cared for him by Merlin's command.

Arthur made great lament when he understood that Sir Ector was not his father. "To you and your wife, my good lady and mother, I owe more than to anyone in the world," he said. "If by God's will I ever become king, ask of me what you will, and I shall not fail you."

Sir Ector said, "I ask only that Sir Kay, your foster brother, be made steward of all your lands."

"That shall be done," said Arthur.

Then they went to the archbishop and told him how Arthur had won the sword. He pulled it from the stone again, while all the barons looked on. But many great lords were angry and said it was a shame that the realm should be governed by a beardless boy of humble birth. Many more great lords came to try for the sword, but none could pull it from the stone. Still they would not acknowledge Arthur as king and said that all must try again at Easter. Once again at Easter, Arthur alone pulled out the sword. Yet even now some of the great lords delayed his coronation.

At last men of all sorts, both high and low, were allowed to try the sword, and none could prevail. But Arthur pulled it out before all the lords and all the common people who were in London. And the common people cried, "We will have Arthur for our king with no more delay. It is God's will that he shall be our king, and we will slay anyone who stands against him."

Then rich and poor knelt down and begged Arthur's forgiveness because they had delayed so long.

Arthur took the sword in both hands and offered it upon the church altar. Then he bathed and kept watch all night before the altar. In the morning he put on a clean white robe and knelt at the feet of Sir Ector, who heard Arthur's vows as a knight: to live a pure life, to speak the truth, to right wrongs. Sir Ector took Arthur's sword in his hands and touched Arthur on the shoulder, saying, "Rise, Sir Arthur. I dub you knight."

Soon afterward Arthur was crowned. He swore that he would be a true king and would stand for justice all the days of his life. From his castle at Camelot he began to right wrongs that had been done since the days of Uther Pendragon. But when he had been crowned, other kings with their hundreds of knights gathered outside his castle, still saying that they refused to be ruled by a beardless boy of low blood. Then Merlin came among them by magic, and they asked him, "Why is that boy Arthur made king?"

"Sirs," said Merlin, "he is Uther Pendragon's son, and whatever you say, he will be king and will overcome all his enemies. Before he dies, he shall be king of all England, Wales, Ireland, and Scotland, and more realms than these. One of his knights will win to the greatest adventure in all the world. He will find the Holy Grail, that long-lost cup from which Our Lord drank at His Last Supper." Then Merlin vanished from their midst and came to Arthur's side. He told Arthur to go out from Camelot and speak to these proud kings, but when he went, they gave him hard words. Some of them prepared to lay siege to his castle, yet many of the best men that were with the kings came to Arthur's side, and that comforted him.

"Sire," said Merlin to Arthur, "do not fight with the sword that you got by miracle until you must. Then draw it and do your best."

And when the kings attacked Arthur's castle from all sides, he drew his sword and went out to meet them. His sword was so bright in his enemies' eyes that it gave light like thirty torches. And the common people arose to help him with clubs and staves, until all the kings and knights who were left alive fled away. Merlin advised Arthur to let them go.

From that time on, Merlin the Magician stood at the king's right hand, warning of dangers, weaving spells from his book of enchantment, and foretelling the future with wisdom beyond that of mortal man. He said that great bards would sing of Arthur in time to come, echoed by old folk at their firesides. They would remember how his helmet with a golden dragon on its crest blazed as he rode to battle. Through Merlin's magic, Arthur's knights saw three fair queens from the Other World who stood behind the throne when the king took his place there. And those closest to him heard soft voices, saying, "We will be with you, Arthur, to help you in your last hour."

So it was that Arthur rode out to unite his kingdom.

TWO

Of Swords and Sorcerers

No king before Arthur had been able to unite the realm and rule it. This Arthur did. Lightnings and thunders surrounded him as he fought. In twelve great battles he defeated petty kings who had been constantly at war, laying waste all the land. The last to surrender was Arthur's own brother-in-law, King Lot of Orkney. When Lot laid down his arms and swore fealty to Arthur, he sent his sons to become knights at Camelot.

One son was Gawain, handsome and strong, whom Arthur called Gawain the Courteous. Another was Mordred, whose foxy smile and gimlet eyes concealed malice and a thirst for power. Gawain took the vows of knighthood in good faith, but Mordred's vows were insincere, and he soon began listening at the castle doors in hope of ferreting out secrets that might damage the court and someday play into his own hands. He saw that the time to strike had not yet come. The powers of heaven and earth all seemed to be on Arthur's side. The people loved him, and Camelot was in its glory.

Now there came a day when Arthur rode with Merlin seeking adventure, and in a forest they found a knight named Pellinore, seated in a chair, blocking their path.

"Sir, will you let us pass?" said Arthur.

"Not without a fight," replied Pellinore. "Such is my custom."

"I will change your custom," said Arthur.

"I will defend it," said Pellinore. He mounted his horse and took his shield on his arm. Then the two knights rode against each other, and each splintered his spear on the other's shield.

"I have no more spears," said Arthur. "Let us fight with swords."

"Not so," said Pellinore. "I have enough spears. I will lend you one."

Then a squire brought two good spears, and the two knights rode against each other again until those spears were broken.

"You are as good a fighter as ever I met," said Pellinore. "Let us try again."

Two great spears were brought, and this time Pellinore struck Arthur's shield so hard that the king and his horse fell to the earth.

Then Arthur pulled out his sword and said, "I have lost the battle on horseback. Let me try you on foot."

Pellinore thought it unfair to attack from his horse, so he dismounted and came toward Arthur with his sword drawn. Then began such a battle that both were covered with blood. After a while they sat down to rest and fought again until both fell to the ground. Again they fought, and the fight was even. But at last Pellinore struck such a blow that Arthur's sword broke into two pieces. Thereupon the king leaped at Pellinore. He threw him down and pulled off his helmet. But Pellinore was a very big man and strong enough to wrestle Arthur under him and pull off the king's helmet. All this time Merlin had watched, silent, but when he saw that Pellinore was about to cut off Arthur's head, he interfered.

"Do not kill this man," he said to Pellinore. "You do not know who he is."

"Why, who is he?" said the knight.

"It is King Arthur," said Merlin.

When he heard this, Pellinore trembled with fear of the royal wrath, for he would not knowingly have fought against the king. Then Merlin cast a spell of sleep on Pellinore so that he fell to the earth as if dead.

"Alas," said Arthur, "you have killed the best knight I ever fought."

"Have no fear," said Merlin. "He will awake in three hours as well as ever he was."

Then he mounted Pellinore's horse and led Arthur to a hermit, who bound up the king's wounds and healed them with good salves, so that he might ride again and go on his way.

But Arthur said, "I have no sword."

"Never fear," said Merlin. "Not far away is a sword that can be yours." So they rode on until they came to a broad lake of clear water. Far out in the middle of the lake Arthur saw an arm clothed in shining white and holding a noble sword, its golden hilt richly set with jewels.

"Lo," said Merlin, "yonder is the sword Excalibur."

Then they saw a lady floating toward them as if she walked on the water. Her garments were like a mist around her.

"That is the Lady of the Lake," said Merlin. "Within the lake is a rock, and within the rock is a palace, and within the palace lives this lady with many other ladies who serve her. She is called Vivien. Speak to her as a friend, and she will give you that sword."

So, when she had come close, Arthur said to her, "Lady, I wish that sword were mine, for I have no sword."

"It shall be yours," said the lady, and she showed Arthur a little boat lying at the edge of the lake. "Row out to the sword," she said. "Take it with its scabbard." Then she disappeared. Arthur and Merlin rowed out into the lake, and Arthur took the sword from the hand that held it. And the arm and the hand vanished under the water.

Arthur and Merlin rowed to shore and went on their way, and whenever Arthur looked on the sword, he liked it well.

"Which do you like better?" asked Merlin. "The sword or the scabbard?"

"I like the sword better," said Arthur.

"The scabbard is worth ten such swords," said Merlin, "for while you wear the scabbard, you will never lose blood, no matter how sorely you are wounded."

So they rode back to Arthur's court, and all his knights marveled when they heard that the king had risked his life in single combat as his poor knights did. They said it was merry to be under such a chieftain.

Not long afterward, Arthur's half sister, Morgan le Fay, a

daughter of his mother, Igraine, came to Camelot. Now Morgan le Fay had been sent to school at a nunnery and had become so learned that she could work magic. She was a witch and was no friend to Arthur. In her heart she plotted the death of the king, for she planned to marry her lover, Sir Accolon of Gaul, and make him king in place of Arthur.

She went to Arthur and said, "My brother, do you trust me?"

"With all my heart," said the king.

"Then lend me your sword and scabbard as a sign of your trust," said Morgan le Fay. "I will return them to you."

Arthur gave her Excalibur with its scabbard. Secretly by enchantment, she made another sword and scabbard like these, and gave them to Arthur. The true Excalibur and its magic scabbard she gave to Accolon. When this was done, Morgan le Fay contrived that Arthur should fight against Accolon, neither one recognizing the other behind their closed visors. To Arthur she only said that he would be doing battle to free many good knights held in prison; and Arthur believed her. She told Accolon that an unknown enemy would come to fight him.

The two knights prepared for combat and rode to face each other from the far ends of a jousting field. They pointed their spears and let their horses run together so fast that each knight struck the other in the middle of his shield and fell to earth, horse and man. Then the two men stood and drew their swords.

But as they fought, Vivien, the Lady of the Lake, all unseen, came into the field, for she knew that Morgan le Fay had plotted for Arthur to be killed that day, and she came to save his life. She watched as the two knights gave many great blows, and always Accolon's sword was stronger than Arthur's. With every blow he wounded Arthur sorely, and blood flowed from every wound.

When Arthur saw how he was bleeding, he knew that his scabbard had been changed by treason, but still he fought, and knightly he endured the pain. Sir Accolon lost no blood and he did not tire, while Arthur grew weaker. With the last of his strength Arthur struck Accolon on the helmet so fiercely that Accolon almost fell to the ground, but with that stroke Arthur's sword broke, leaving him with only the hilt in his hand.

Sir Accolon said, "Knight, you are overcome. Yield before I slay you."

Even then, full of valor, Arthur would not yield and still pressed forward. Accolon struck back, but as he struck, the Lady of the Lake caused Excalibur to fall from his hand. Arthur leaped to pick it up, and the moment he had it in his hand, he knew it was Excalibur. Then he spied the scabbard hanging by Accolon's side, and seized it from him. He threw it as far as he could throw and rushed on Accolon with all his might, giving him a great blow on the head and pulling off the helmet. Then he recognized Accolon, one of his own knights, and asked, "Who gave you that sword?"

Accolon said, "Sir, because of that sword, I am about to die. Now at death's door, I must tell the truth." Then he confessed Morgan le Fay's whole plot.

As Accolon fell silent, Arthur raised his helmet, and Accolon saw that he had fought against his king.

"Sire, have mercy on me," he cried. "I did not know who you were."

"You shall have mercy," said Arthur. "You are a traitor, but I blame you less than my half sister, Morgan le Fay, whom I trusted more than anyone in the world."

There was a rich abbey three miles away, and King Arthur and Sir Accolon were carried to it so that their wounds could be cared for. Sir Accolon died within four days from loss of blood, but King Arthur's wounds healed quickly. He sent Accolon's body to Morgan le Fay with a message: "I have my sword Excalibur and the scabbard."

Now Morgan le Fay was wild with anger at the death of her lover, Sir Accolon, and she determined to destroy the king. She came by night to the room where Arthur was asleep and looked for Excalibur and its magic scabbard. But Arthur slept with his sword close by his side. She could not take it without waking him. Then she saw the scabbard lying on the floor, and she hid it under her cloak and was gone. She rode off on horseback a great distance until she came to a deep lake. She threw the scabbard into the middle of the lake, where it sank at once, for it was heavy with gold and precious stones.

The scabbard was never seen again, and from that time on, King Arthur could be wounded like any other man.

THREE

Of Guinevere
and the Round Table

One day soon after his struggle with Accolon, Arthur was overcome by a great weariness. At a small forest hermitage near the city of Cameliard, he stopped for some days to rest before riding on to Camelot.

A young gentlewoman with her serving women came to tend him there. She brought healing herbs and rich food and cared for him so well that she seemed to him an angel. But the king was weak, his ears still full of the hoofbeats of horses and the clash of sword on shield, so that he did not speak to her.

It was as he rode homeward toward Camelot, strength renewed, that he asked his companions, "Who was that lady?"

"Sire, she was the Princess Guinevere," the knights replied. "She is the daughter of Leodegrance of Cameliard, the good king to whom your father Uther gave the famous Round Table."

"Truly the princess is kind and beautiful," Arthur said.

But, greatly as he admired her, his mind was to be for some time full of other matters. When he reached Camelot, he found the court in disarray. Knights who had won splendid victories were now quarreling over who had shown the greatest valor in the wars and who deserved a place near to the king at his banquet table.

Those who were forced by their companions to sit at the far end of the table, either because of youth or lowly birth or some imagined lack of courage, were fiery with anger. Some even threatened to leave Camelot and go their separate ways.

By showing love and respect for all, Arthur was able to end the open quarreling, but the peace of the court was still uneasy.

Now Merlin, as was his way in time of trouble, appeared before the king.

"It is time for this land to have a queen, Sire. Your knights would wish this," he said. "Is there any lady who pleases you?"

Arthur remembered the beautiful visitor who had come to tend him in his weariness.

"There is a lady who pleases me very much," he said. "She is the princess Guinevere, daughter of King Leodegrance of Cameliard."

"There are other princesses who are more kind and loyal," Merlin replied. "I would not choose Guinevere, for I foresee that she may one day do you a great harm so that your kingdom itself could be destroyed. Yet once you have set your heart upon one lady, Sire, I think that you will not draw back."

"I will not draw back," said Arthur. "But the princess Guinevere must not be forced to become my wife. I will ask King Leodegrance for his daughter's hand only when she herself freely grants it to me. Help me by your magic, Merlin. Help me to win my bride."

So Merlin made a magic plan, and in furtherance of that plan the king with a small number of his best knights rode to a castle a short distance from the stronghold of Leodegrance. There he left his companions, his white horse, and his armor and set out on foot for Cameliard. On his head he wore a tattered black cap which Merlin had given him, and that cap by the magician's power had transformed Arthur into a simple gardener's boy.

In this disguise he knocked at the gates of Cameliard and begged employment in the garden of the princess Guinevere. Through Merlin's cunning, the head gardener had that very day lost his assistant. Since it was high summer and there was much work to be done among the flowers, he promptly hired the stranger.

The next morning the princess Guinevere came out to walk in the garden with her ladies. She saw the new gardener's boy bent over the roses and felt a strange pang that she did not herself understand.

Truly I have known that boy, she thought.

The next morning she came early to the garden and walked closer to him.

On the third morning she and her ladies met the boy face-to-face upon the path.

"Saucy youth, why do you not take off your cap before the princess Guinevere?" her ladies protested.

"I cannot take off my cap," the gardener's boy answered.

The ladies gabbled angrily, but the princess made excuse. "Let the boy be," she said. "It may be he is ashamed of some mark upon his head."

So matters might have gone on, with Guinevere walking daily

· 23 ·

in her garden or looking down from a castle balcony, the gardener's boy aware of her gaze. But at dusk on that third day a knight, all dusty and damp with travel, came galloping into Cameliard.

"A warning! A warning!" he shouted. "King Ryence of North Wales is marching upon you with a large army. He means to capture the castle and to carry away the princess Guinevere as his bride."

The alarm rang along the castle halls. Everywhere were fear and consternation. King Leodegrance was a good king but growing old and no longer a great warrior. In these last years his strongest knights had fallen in battle or gone to join younger and more powerful lords.

"Who is there left to defend us?" the people cried, while the king himself sat despairing in an inner room.

No one saw the boy in the black cap slip out of the castle garden at nightfall and make his way alone into the dark.

The next morning a knight in white armor came riding up to Cameliard upon a snowy stallion. This knight did not carry a pennant or wear any kind of emblem upon his shield. But he brandished a jeweled sword, and he rode toward the field where King Ryence of North Wales had assembled his forces. There one of King Ryence's knights, the giant duke of Northumberland, rode arrogantly up and down, challenging any follower of King Leodegrance to come joust with him.

"Are you all such weaklings and cowards that you do not dare to meet me?" he thundered.

At sight of that challenger the newly appeared knight spurred his white stallion fearlessly, though Northumberland seemed in that morning's brilliant sunlight to be fifteen feet tall. The stranger knight rode to the castle balcony where the princess Guinevere stood pale with terror. At the foot of the balcony he called up to her through his visor.

"I beg you, beautiful lady, give me the pearl necklace that you wear. I shall carry it into battle against this duke of Northumberland, and I promise you to fight with him as long as I have breath."

Now the princess Guinevere thought the voice from the visor was almost certainly one she knew. She found strength to unclasp her pearl necklace and drop it over the edge of her balcony. The stranger knight caught the necklace upon the tip of his sword, twisted it about his wrist, and so turned to attack the giant who rushed toward him.

It was a cruel combat, the two riders plunging up and down the field, swords flashing, dust flying, and the earth itself shuddering under the hoofbeats of the horses. After hours of fierce struggle, the duke of Northumberland at last tired. The stranger knight with a powerful thrust drove his sword between the giant's helmet and the breastplate of his armor so that his head was more than half cut off.

At that sight shouts rose from the castle. Knights of King Leodegrance, who had up to now feared to risk their lives, suddenly burst forth onto the field and fell upon the army of King Ryence.

The men of that army were so surprised by the unexpected attack and the bloody death of their champion that they broke ranks and fled.

When Leodegrance's victorious knights looked for their deliv-

erer, he too had gone. The starlit night gave back no echo of him.

Early the next morning, the princess Guinevere hurried to look down again into her garden and saw the gardener's boy wearing his black cap among the roses. She was filled with gratitude toward him but did not dare speak of what she guessed.

"Alas, you are not yet saved, daughter," her father said. "None of us is saved. One defeat will not long turn away King Ryence. He will come again tomorrow. Who will protect us for a second time?"

The princess Guinevere did not answer, but that night at dusk, when she looked down into her garden, she saw a tattered black cap lying among the flowers. Despite her father's despairing words, her heart was strangely light.

The next morning King Ryence regrouped his forces, as King Leodegrance had predicted. The Welsh knights stood on the far side of the field facing Cameliard with banners flying, swords and spears jostling, and war horns sounding loud. King Ryence himself shouted a mocking challenge.

"Where is your knight-without-an-emblem today, cowards of Cameliard?"

Then, as the Welsh war steeds neighed restlessly and the banners flapped in the breeze, yet another group of knights appeared in the distance, half-hidden by the cloud of dust which came with them in a brown billow along the road.

Although they were not so many as the Welshmen, these new knights rode fearlessly and soon plunged out onto the field. At their head was yesterday's knight on the snow-white stallion, the pearl necklace of the princess Guinevere bound about his wrist.

If the first combat had been fearsome, this one was so violent and bloody that few on the castle balconies could bear to look upon it. Blood flowed so freely as to make a scarlet carpet. Men were thrown from their mounts onto that slippery mat and, heavy with armor, could not rise. No squires could come to help their lords through the flying blows. The air rang with moans and sobs.

At the height of the battle, knights and horses alike vanished into a swirling mist sent by Merlin himself to blind the Welsh army.

When that magic mist was lifted, all fighting was at an end. Watchers from the castle saw that many Welsh knights lay dead upon the ground. Others limped or crawled from the field. Still others had already fled, leaving their banners and weapons and their fallen war-horses behind them. The defenders of Cameliard were entirely victorious.

That night King Leodegrance gave a feast of thanksgiving, and on that night the champion who had ridden the white stallion came into the banquet hall. Guinevere's pearl necklace was bound to his right wrist, the ragged cap of the gardener's boy bound to his left. Courteously he went to where the princess Guinevere was seated. He knelt down before her and flung back his helmet so that the two looked into each other's eyes.

"It is my faithful gardener's boy," Guinevere cried. "And it is King Arthur!"

"How do you know this, daughter?" King Leodegrance demanded.

"Because I tended him last year when he rested nearby in the forest. I could not forget his face."

"Nor I yours, lady," Arthur said. "I shall not forget you till the day I die. Nor would I, for all the world, have let King Ryence carry you away. I beg you, if you and your good father are willing, be my lady wife."

"I am most willing, my lord Arthur," Guinevere replied.

The knights of Cameliard were overjoyed to recognize their high king. Leodegrance welcomed him royally and freely granted him his daughter's hand.

"I will give you a wedding gift, Sire, such as king never had before," Leodegrance said. "It is the Round Table made for your father, Uther, by Merlin the Magician many years ago. There are one hundred and fifty places at that table, and one hundred and fifty chairs set about it. All are yours. Remember this thing, Sire. One of these chairs is called the Siege Perilous—the seat of danger. Merlin has prophesied that only he who is the purest and best of all knights on earth, he who will one day see the Holy Grail, can sit upon that chair. If any other try it, he will surely come to harm."

For a moment Arthur shivered at that warning, but when he was led to the Round Table, he saw that it was very beautiful, for it was cunningly crafted of marble and ebony. The chairs also were ebony, and Leodegrance said that by magic a name would appear in letters of gold upon the back of each seat when the knight for whom it was destined came to claim it.

Arthur hoped that there would no longer be any quarreling among his companions. At the Round Table each would have an equal place, excepting only for the king's high seat and for two others. "The greatest knight in all the realm—when he has by valor proven himself to be so—will sit at my left hand. The Siege Perilous will be at my right," Arthur said. So he was filled with joy both because of the bride he had won and because of the magic gift.

For her part, the princess Guinevere kept the gardener boy's black cap until the song-sweet morning when she rode into Camelot to celebrate her wedding day.

FOUR

Of True Love

To be a knight of King Arthur's Round Table was the greatest honor that could come to any man. It was no easy thing to deserve that honor. Each year, at the Feast of Pentecost, Arthur's knights renewed their vows to live pure lives, to speak the truth, to fight for the right, and to be faithful to the king. Always faithful to his word, Arthur believed that his knights would keep the vows they had made, and he waited for that perfect knight who, as Merlin had prophesied, would find the Holy Grail. As yet no knight of the Round Table was worthy to scc that gracious cup.

One year, at Pentecost, not long after the founding of the Round Table, Vivien, the Lady of the Lake, rode into Arthur's great hall, followed by a young squire who rode his horse like a knight and looked about him as if he had lived at court all his life. At the king's feet he leaped from his horse and dropped to his knees.

"My lord king," said the lady Vivien, "this is Lancelot. Merlin brought him from his birthplace in France to be trained for knighthood in my lake palace, prophesying that he would be peerless in all the qualities of knighthood. He is called Lancelot of the Lake. Knight him, my lord, for he is worthy to take his place at your Round Table."

Arthur looked at Lancelot, and his heart warmed to him. He drew Excalibur from its scabbard and lightly touched the young man on the shoulder. Lancelot took the vows of knighthood. "Rise, Sir Lancelot," said Arthur. "Take your place."

Now two of the seats at the Round Table were empty and were covered with veils, awaiting the day when knights should come who were worthy to sit there. One was the Siege Perilous. The other was the chair at the king's left hand.

Lancelot walked to this seat. "For what else was I born?" he said. He drew aside the veil, and behold, his name, Lancelot, appeared in letters of gold on the back of that seat, and he sat there. The lady Vivien went away.

But some of the knights muttered among themselves, "We have earned our seats here. The king honors this stranger before he has been tested."

Then Guinevere entered the great hall with her ladies, and Lancelot saw her. She was the fairest lady on earth, he thought. All the beauty and grace under heaven were in the light of her eyes. Alas, she was the queen, wife of the king to whom this very day he had pledged his loyalty. Yet it was Lancelot's fate that from that moment she was the only woman he could love, even though he knew that death and dishonor might come of it. He swore in his heart to be her knight champion as long as he might live and to serve her at all costs. Yet he must also faithfully serve his lord.

Before many days had passed, Lancelot was known as the best of the king's knights. Few men dared oppose him in armed combat and of those who did, fewer lived to tell the tale. It pleased the queen that Lancelot, who could rule all men, was ruled by her, both when she smiled and when she frowned upon him. She showed him a ring that she often wore and said, "If ever I need you, I will send you this." Arthur was not unwilling that Lancelot should pledge himself to the queen's service. There were also others always about her, called the Queen's Knights, who carried pure white shields, and Arthur trusted to their care the safety of his well-loved queen.

One day, as Lancelot rode out from Camelot, adventuring, he came to a high and lonely castle where an old king, Pelles, lived with his daughter Elaine. Now there was a prophecy that the best of Arthur's knights would be the father of a son born to Elaine. Lancelot's name and fame had traveled before him, and when Pelles saw him and heard his name, he believed that this was the knight who was meant to wed Elaine. Pelles wished it to happen, and Elaine fell deeply in love with Lancelot at first sight, but it was well known that Lancelot served no lady in the world except Queen Guinevere.

A lady of the castle, an enchantress named Brison, said secretly to Pelles, "Leave it all to me. I will cast a spell, and Lancelot shall think that the queen has called him to her for love's sake. He has never yet kissed the queen, but now he will forget his vows of knighthood. Tonight the lady Elaine must go to your little castle at Case, and all will be as you wish."

When Elaine had gone to the appointed place, Brison sent a messenger to Lancelot with a ring like the one the queen wore. Lancelot followed the messenger to the Castle of Case, and there he saw knights and ladies who seemed to him like those who attended Guinevere. Then Brison gave him a cup of wine, a potion that she had made by enchantment, and led him to a chamber where a lady was waiting for him. In the darkness it seemed to Lancelot that he saw Guinevere coming to him with looks of love.

Then Lancelot did indeed forget his vow to be faithful to King Arthur in every way. He took the lady in his arms and made love to her as if she were Guinevere, and the lady Elaine was glad, for she knew that Lancelot would beget a son, who would be the best knight in the world.

But in the morning, the enchantment was past. Lancelot saw beside him not Guinevere but Elaine, and he knew that he had sinned against his king and queen and against the lady Elaine.

"Alas," he said to her, "I am ashamed because of you."

Then Elaine knelt before Lancelot and said, "What has happened was prophesied. It was my fate to love you, and I shall bear your child."

Lancelot kissed her in farewell, saying, "You are not to blame. I am to blame—I, and the witch who put the enchantment on me." And he went away from the little Castle of Case.

For many months Lancelot did not return to King Arthur's court, but wandered in the forest without armor or weapons, out of his mind with grief and shame at his faithlessness. At last he could suffer no more and fell into a long sleep. When he awoke he found that he had returned to the Castle of Case, and there Elaine tenderly nursed him back to health. She told him that their child, Galahad, had been born and was in the care of nuns who would teach him the good things he needed to know for the life he was to lead.

In time Elaine gave Lancelot a horse and armor and sent him on his way to Camelot, for she knew that he would never love her as she loved him.

King Arthur received Lancelot with joy as he again took his seat at the Round Table, and Gawain welcomed him like a brother. But other knights were still jealous of Lancelot's fame as the best of all King Arthur's knights. One of these was Mordred, who was said to be the son of Morgan le Fay, the enchantress. She hated Arthur, her half brother. Mordred too hated the king. He saw a way to bring about the end of King Arthur's reign and to seize the throne for himself. So he spread false rumors through the court that Lancelot and Guinevere were guilty lovers who had betrayed the king's trust. But Arthur believed that the queen was true to him, and at the same time he trusted Mordred as he trusted Lancelot, for both had taken the vows of knighthood to live pure lives, to speak the truth, to right wrongs, and to follow the king.

As for Lancelot himself, whenever any knight or lady of the court whispered that the queen was unfaithful to her lord King Arthur, Lancelot fought to defend her fair name. Often he was sorely wounded, but in the end no knight could stand against him. Always in these combats he carried the plain white shield of a Queen's Knight, or some other shield not his own so that no one knew who he was. Always, when he had won the victory, he rode away from the field without raising his visor.

Now it happened that King Arthur was in London with his queen and some chosen knights, and he planned a great tournament to be held in the summer at Camelot. He invited many famous knights to come from all over the kingdom. But Queen Guinevere said that she was sick and could not ride to Camelot at that time. Arthur was sorry, for he wanted her to see him jousting with other knights. Lancelot told the king that he could not go to fight in the tournament at Camelot because he had received a wound that was not yet healed. Then Guinevere called Lancelot to her privately and said, "You must fight in this tournament or our enemies will say that we have been together while the king was absent."

"Madam," said Lancelot, "I will obey you, and I will take what comes."

As he rode toward Camelot, he came to an ancient castle and asked for a night's lodging. The castle stood at the edge of a river and an old baron named Sir Bernard lived there with his sons and a daughter. The place was called Astolat. The baron's daughter was named Elaine. She was so lovely to look upon that she was known as the Fair Maid of Astolat, but Lancelot, looking at her, showed only knightly courtesy, remembering that other Elaine.

While Sir Bernard and Sir Lancelot talked about the coming tournament, Elaine went to and fro, and each time she looked at her father's guest, she loved him more and more, for he was the noblest knight she had ever seen. Before they parted for the night, she begged Lancelot to tie around his helmet a scarlet sleeve from her dress, embroidered with pearls, as a token that he fought with her favor and her blessing.

Lancelot had never before worn a token from any lady, but to please her in all courtesy, he agreed. When the day came for the great tournament, Lancelot left his own shield at Astolat. Elaine's brother Lavaine gave him a white shield much like those the Queen's Knights wore, and they rode away to Camelot.

There before a great company of people Lancelot jousted against one knight after another with a right good will. Always he won, and all wondered at his strength and valor.

"Yonder knight fights like Lancelot," Sir Gawain said to the king. "But it cannot be Lancelot. He has never worn a lady's token."

At last, three knights charged at Sir Lancelot all together. They struck his horse to the ground, and a spear pierced through his shield so that it broke, leaving the iron spearhead in Lancelot's side. Lavaine brought him another spear and shield and helped him to mount a fresh horse. Then Lancelot fought back against those three knights so fiercely that he knocked off their helmets, and he would have slain them. But when he saw their faces, he spared them because they were knights of the Round Table. That day, it is said, Lancelot struck down more than thirty knights.

When the great tournament ended, the trumpets blew, and King Arthur's heralds gave the prize to the knight with the white shield, wearing a lady's sleeve tied around his helmet. Then Lancelot left the field quickly with Lavaine. When he was sure that he would not be seen, he dismounted and said to Lavaine, "Take this spearhead out of my side, or I must die." And Lavaine obeyed, though in great fear as blood burst from the wound.

They rode at full speed to a hermitage not far off where a hermit lived who had once been a knight of the Round Table. He knew Lancelot at once and skillfully set about to stanch the blood and heal the deep wound.

Now King Arthur sent Gawain to search for the unknown knight who had won the tournament, and as Gawain rode, he came to Astolat. There he told how the victor was a knight who wore a lady's scarlet sleeve on his helmet.

"Now blessed be God," said the Fair Maid of Astolat. "That knight is the first man I have ever loved and he shall be the last."

"Do you know his name?" said Sir Gawain.

Then Lavaine said, "His name is Lancelot." He told where he had left Lancelot sorely wounded, and Elaine went to the hermitage and nursed Lancelot day and night, most tenderly.

King Arthur was holding court in London when Gawain returned to him, bringing news that the victor at the tournament was Lancelot, who had worn the scarlet sleeve. Gawain also told how Elaine loved Lancelot and was nursing him back to health. But Queen Guinevere was angrier than she had ever been in her life. Word of her anger came to Lancelot as he made ready to leave the hermitage, restored to health and strength. I was not at fault, he thought. I did nothing to win the love of this fair maid. Then he said to Elaine, "I must go back to King Arthur's court. Take a husband and be happy. I will never marry, but I will give a thousand pounds a year for you and your children." Elaine turned away, and wept. Within a few days Lancelot had left her.

In London all the knights of the Round Table welcomed him with joy, excepting those who were jealous of him. Queen Guinevere would not speak to him.

The Fair Maid of Astolat was so sorrowful that she could neither eat nor sleep, and she knew that she would soon die. Then she said to her father and her brother, "Write what I tell you, and when I am dead, put the letter in my hand. Carry me to the river Thames and put me in a black boat that you will find there. Let a trusted servant row the boat down the river to London." All this was done.

It happened that King Arthur and Queen Guinevere were standing together at a window and saw the black boat, and they went with all the court to see what this strange thing was. There they saw a fair young woman, lying richly dressed in cloth of gold, with a letter in her hand. Strangely, she seemed to smile.

The king opened the letter which was brought to him and had it read aloud: "I am Elaine of Astolat. You did not love me, Sir Lancelot, but I died for love of you, because you are peerless. Pray for my soul."

Then Arthur sent for Sir Lancelot and had the letter read to him. "She was both fair and good," said Lancelot, "and I am grieved that she is dead. But love cannot be commanded. It comes from the heart."

The next morning he ordered a solemn funeral for Elaine, the Fair Maid of Astolat, and she was buried with all honors. The queen begged Lancelot to forgive her for her anger, though it was not the first time she had been angry with him who was always true to her.

FIVE

Of the Sword Bridge

T he month of May came, the loveliest month in the year, when the world is once more in blossom and hearts are young again, remembering old loves and long-forgotten kindnesses. And Queen Guinevere rode with ten knights and ten ladies to gather May flowers in the fields and woods. Each knight wore green in honor of May Day and carried no weapon but a light sword. Sir Lancelot was not with them.

Now there was a wicked knight named Sir Malagant who had been in love with Queen Guinevere for many years and had plotted to steal her away if he could find her unprotected. So as Queen Guinevere rode merrily with her knights and ladies, their arms full of flowers, suddenly Sir Malagant attacked them with a great troop of heavily armed men. The Queen's Knights fought valiantly to defend her, but when she saw that, so lightly armed, they would all be killed, she cried, "Stop, Sir Malagant. I will go with you, if you will spare the lives of my knights."

Sir Malagant was well pleased and led all the company away to his castle, for he wanted no word of this attack to reach the king's court. But there was a young boy with the queen, and she spoke secretly to him. "When you see a chance, ride and take this ring to Sir Lancelot. Tell him to rescue me, if he loves me." The boy set spurs to his horse and rode off. Sir Malagant saw him and sent men to shoot him down with bows and arrows, but he escaped. He carried the queen's ring to Sir Lancelot, telling him where the queen had been attacked and how she was now held captive by the evil Sir Malagant.

Sir Lancelot set off at once and came to the place where the Queen's Knights had fought. There Sir Malagant had left thirty archers to lie treacherously in wait for Lancelot, who would surely come. "Shoot his horse," Sir Malagant had said, "but do not attack Lancelot himself. He is too strong for you."

When the archers ordered Lancelot to turn back, he scorned them, saying, "Bows and arrows are the weapons of cowards."

When he came on, the archers shot his horse with many arrows, so that it fell down. Still Lancelot went forward on foot at full speed, and put so many hedges and ditches between him and the archers that they soon lost sight of him. And all the while, his horse followed.

Now Lancelot's armor and shield and spear were heavy, even for a man of his strength, and when he saw a man driving a cartload of wood, he called, "Will you take me to the castle of Sir Malagant?"

"I am going there," said the carter. "Climb in." It was a cart such as a common criminal would ride in to go to his hanging, but Lancelot stepped into it. He was ashamed, yet it would be a greater shame if he failed to rescue the queen. So he rode on until the cart reached a town where even the common people shouted, "Who is this man riding in a hangman's cart? Is he a robber or a murderer?"

The greatest knight at King Arthur's court bore their insults without a word. At last he came to a tower where a young girl looked down from a high window.

"Where do you go," she called, "riding in a hangman's cart and with your horse full of arrows?"

"I go to the castle of Sir Malagant," said Lancelot.

"That is hard to do," said the girl. "The castle is surrounded by a bottomless sea. Malagant and his friends are rowed to and from the castle, but for his enemies there are only two ways to enter. One is by a water bridge, deep under the sea where a knight in armor would surely drown. The other is a sword bridge, and no one has ever crossed it for fear of quick death."

"I will cross it," said Lancelot.

"Then dismount from that cart and leave your horse with me," said the girl. "I will care for it, and I will give you another horse. God be with you." She took him into her tower and gave him food and drink and a fresh mount before she would let him go on his way.

Lancelot rode then until he came to the end of the land. There he saw Malagant's castle towering above dark water, and the sword bridge, as long as three lances, stretching ahead of him, sharp and shining. He pulled off his gauntlets and his armor-clad boots because they would slip against the steel. He strapped

his shield and sword to his back. Then, on his hands and knees, he crossed the sword bridge. Blood poured from his wounds, but on he went, hand over hand, foot by bloody foot, until he reached the castle. While he stood there, wiping his wounds as best he might, Malagant came to the gateway.

"I know well that you have come to rescue the queen," he said. "I believe that she is unfaithful to her lord King Arthur, and I have sent a messenger to tell him so. But I will be more than fair. You shall see the queen and her companions, and then I will send them home. You, too, return to Camelot. I swear to meet you in battle in one week's time. If you do not come to face me in combat that day, all will know that the queen is false, a traitor to her lord."

Malagant guided Lancelot through the castle as if to take him to Queen Guinevere. Now in a certain chamber there was a trap in the floor, and Lancelot, walking where Malagant pointed the way, stepped on the trap. He fell sixty feet into a dungeon, and there he lay.

Well pleased with his plot to torment and humiliate the king and queen, Sir Malagant went on to the hall where Guinevere and her ladies were tending her wounded knights.

"Madam," said Malagant, "Sir Lancelot has come to this castle and has gone away as suddenly as he came. He has sworn to meet me in battle at Camelot a week from today to defend your honor against the charge of treason. If he does not come, you will be judged guilty in the eyes of all the world. If he comes, and I am the victor, the king will have you burned at the stake, as the law allows, or he will give you to me. Now you shall be rowed across the water and will find your horses waiting for you."

Guinevere and her company returned to Camelot, but Lancelot was nowhere to be seen, and as one day followed another, the queen was ill at ease.

The king sought to reassure her.

"Malagant has taken much on himself to accuse you of treason, my lady," he said. "Have no fear. Lancelot will come and will kill Malagant for his foul words. I know that Lancelot is true to you, his sovereign lady, and to me, his king."

Meanwhile, day after day Lancelot lay in pain on the floor of Malagant's dungeon. He would have died but that a lady brought him food and drink, and each day she said to him, "Sir Lancelot, I will help you escape if you will be my love."

"That I cannot do," he said.

"Sir Lancelot," said she, "you are not wise, for if you do not escape, you will die here, and Sir Malagant will take the queen for himself."

"If I do not come, my friends will know that I am either dead or in prison, and someone will fight in my place," said Lancelot. "I mean no discourtesy, but I will not make love to you."

"Then you will be destroyed," said the lady. Yet on the day set for battle she came to him and said, "Sir Lancelot, you are too hard-hearted. But kiss me once, and I will help you escape and give you new armor and the best horse in Malagant's stable."

"I will kiss you gladly," said Lancelot. "A kiss is no disgrace." Then he kissed her and she let him out of the dungeon and sent him on his way, clad in shining armor and mounted on a white steed with spear in hand and sword by his side. "Lady," he said, as he set forth, "for this good deed I will never forget you."

In Camelot the field was prepared for combat and Arthur sat with Queen Guinevere and all his knights and ladies around him. Trumpets sounded as Malagant rode to one end of the field. He called for Lancelot, but there was no answer. Again he called.

"My lord Arthur," said Sir Lavaine, who loved Lancelot well, "let me fight in Lancelot's place for the honor of the queen."

"I give you leave," said the king. "Lancelot must have met with treason, or else he is dead."

Then Malagant called out a third time, and Lavaine rode to the other end of the field to do battle for the queen's honor. But as the heralds were about to call, "Ready! Ride!" a knight galloped in at full speed, riding on a white charger. It was Lancelot.

"Ho! Wait!" cried Arthur, and he called Lancelot to him. Then Lancelot told in the hearing of everyone what Malagant had done from first to last. And Queen Guinevere watched at the king's side while Lancelot prepared to do battle.

There was nothing more to be said. Sir Lancelot and Sir Malagant faced each other. They took their spears in hand and came together with a sound like thunder. The first thrust of Lancelot's spear threw Malagant backward off his horse. Then Lancelot leaped from his own horse and ran toward Malagant with his sword drawn. They smote each other with many great blows, until Malagant fell to the ground again, and all expected Lancelot to kill him then and there.

But Lancelot said, "Stand, traitor, and I will fight you without my helmet or the armor on my left side. I will fight you with my left hand tied behind my back."

Then Sir Lancelot's helmet was taken off and half his armor, and his left hand was tied behind him so that he could not carry his shield. Fully armed, Malagant rushed upon Lancelot, who met him with his head and half his body unarmed. So the two fought again, blow for blow, while all the knights and ladies marveled at Lancelot's valor as he turned Malagant's thrusts aside and skillfully struck with his own sword. At last he struck such a blow that it severed Malagant's helmet from top to bottom and split his head. He was carried from the field, dead and in disgrace.

Arthur decreed that words should be written in stone above Malagant's grave, telling who slew him and why he was slain. And the king loved and cherished Lancelot of the Lake more than ever. He gave him a castle in the north, called Joyous Gard, because he had fought for the honor of Queen Guinevere.

But Lancelot saw ahead of him one struggle that he might never win—the fight to be true to King Arthur and also true to the queen, whom both of them loved.

SIX

Of the Boy
Who Would Be a Knight

During these years there lived in a wild forest in Wales a great lady, sister to King Uther Pendragon who had died. By her own choice this lady stayed in hiding with one son, one old servant woman, and a flock of white goats to furnish milk and meat and skins for garments.

The lady's son was named Percival. His father had been a noble knight who had been killed in battle along with his two older sons. The murderer—for the deaths had been brought about by treachery, not in fair combat—was known as the Red Knight.

Determined not to lose her last dear child to this wicked swordsman or to any other, the lady had carried the baby Percival into the wilderness where he would never hear of war or clash of arms.

Percival himself knew nothing of his own story. His boyhood was a happy one. He grew up tall and strong and handsome and supposed that everyone in the world—if there was a world beyond his forest—was like himself.

His mother taught the boy peaceable games such as chess and all manner of useful knowledge, about the birds and wild-flowers and the turning of the seasons, about the good God and how to say his prayers. She told him strange tales of a mystic cup and a spear. From his early years she let him roam the forest freely. There, with the help of a small spear which had been his father's, he became an excellent huntsman. His eye was as sharp as a falcon's, and he ran more swiftly than the fallow deer.

One morning when he was fifteen years old, Percival heard an unfamiliar sound in the forest, neither birdsong nor blowing wind. It rang in his ears more sweetly even than the music his mother made in the evenings upon her harp.

At once he set off through the woody underbrush until he saw in the distance five figures in sun-glinting garments. The strangers were mounted upon great panting animals who wore what seemed to be flowing skirts, all jeweled and multicolored.

Percival rushed breathlessly home.

"Tell me who are these beings I have seen in the forest, Mother!" he demanded.

The lady's heart turned over once in fear, and she said, "These were angels, my son. Do not trouble them."

Percival had never before disobeyed his mother, but neither had he been filled with such strange longing. The next morning he hurried back into the forest and saw again the five marvelous beings. This time he ran directly to the foremost of them, who, he saw, was awaiting him.

"My mother says that you are angels," Percival gasped, and fell upon his knees. "I think you must be gods."

"Rise to your feet, lad," the stranger replied kindly. "We are not gods. Nor are we angels. We are knights of King Arthur's court. My name is Gawain."

All that meant nothing to Percival who had never until the day before seen a knight or until this moment heard of Arthur's court.

"What are these great animals you are riding and the skirts they wear?" he demanded.

"These are war-horses, richly caparisoned, as is fitting for them," Sir Gawain said.

"But what are those strange hats you wear upon your heads?" Percival persisted. "And what are those great platters hung upon your arms?"

Now Sir Gawain had long been noted in Arthur's court for his courteous tongue. Very gravely and patiently he named his helmet and shield. He named also his sword and lance and saddle and all the splendid trappings upon his horse.

"I, too, will be a knight!" Percival declared.

"Then you must come to Arthur's court at Camelot and do noble deeds in his name. It is he who will knight you when you have earned that honor," Sir Gawain said, and the five knights rode away, their bright armor jingling.

Percival rushed home again.

"Those were not angels, Mother!" he cried. "They were knights of King Arthur's court, and I am going to follow them."

At first the lady wept bitterly. Then she told Percival the story of his dead father and brothers and warned him of the perils that would threaten him in the wide world. But after a while she saw that his mind was made up, and she gave him the diamond ring from her finger and granted him permission to go.

"Remember always that you are of noble lineage. Keep good company," she bade him. "If you are hungry, get what you need to eat and drink. Take no more than a single kiss from a beautiful maiden, except that you may take her ring also if you give her your own. Help those in need. At every church door stop to pray. If somewhere in the great world you meet your uncle, my only living brother, trust him and accept his aid. He is an old and honorable knight."

So Percival whittled out of wood a coat of armor which seemed to him like that armor Sir Gawain and his companions had worn, and he put it on over his goatskin garments. He took a pack upon his back and set off running through the forest.

On the second evening he came to a rapidly flowing stream. Pitched beside it was an azure tent which seemed to him so splendid that he thought it must be a church, and he knelt down to pray.

But when he rose to his feet again, he saw beyond the tent flap a table set with wine and fresh-roasted boar meat and bread. In two days running he had had nothing to eat except a few scraps of cold food which the old servant woman had put into his pack, and he was very hungry. Remembering his mother's bidding, he went inside the tent and ate and drank.

When he had finished the meal, he saw that a young woman stood watching him. Her eyes were as blue as chicory petals and her skin as white as campion flowers. He had never imagined that any woman could be so beautiful. Before she could protest—though indeed she did not seem to mind—he kissed her lips and took from her finger her gold ring with its ruby stone. Upon her finger he placed in return the diamond ring his mother had given him.

"What is your name, beautiful lady?" he asked.

"I am Blanchefleur, Lady of the White Flower," she answered. "I have never met a lad as handsome as you. But I must warn you that you are in grave danger. I hear my brothers and their men-at-arms returning. They will be very angry if they find you here."

"I do not like to leave you," Percival protested.

"Go! There is a pony tethered out beside the stream. Take her and ride as quickly as you can," the lady ordered. "Dusk is falling, and my brothers will not see you in the shadows."

Percival reluctantly untethered the waiting pony, folded his pack for a saddle, and, though he had never ridden before, galloped away into the dark. The next morning he took twigs and reeds and wove a kind of armor for the pony.

Then, stopping here and there to eat and to ask directions, he journeyed on toward King Arthur's court.

He came to the city of Camelot on a golden afternoon when the king, with Sir Gawain and other knights, had gone out hunting. A great number of the king's subjects, finely dressed, thronged the narrow streets within the city walls. Some laughed and pointed their fingers at Percival in his strange attire, but he did not doubt that he would be welcome at the king's court.

Right into the great banquet hall of the castle he rode upon his pony.

"Ho! See what we have here!" cried a short, puffy-cheeked knight who came strutting toward him. "Has someone been emptying out his stables and sent us the sweepings?"

The rude words were scarcely spoken when a knight in glittering red armor strode after Percival into the banquet hall. As all eyes turned toward him, the newcomer went to a small table where a page boy was pouring a goblet of wine for Queen Guinevere. With his mailed fist he knocked at the page boy's elbow so that the wine flew into the queen's face and wet her silken gown. Then he seized the queen's golden goblet and strode away with it, shouting as he went, "Let anyone who dares follow and challenge me."

There was a stunned silence in the hall until one knight demanded, "Who will avenge this insult to the queen?"

Silence fell again. It was clear that none of those present wished to rush to combat. They were not cowardly men, but the insult seemed to them so shocking that they thought the Red Knight must be protected by magic which they could not defeat.

It was the boy Percival, ignorant of all such fears, who declared, "I will ride after that wicked man. I will make him pay for his discourtesy to the queen, and I will win back the golden goblet. My mother told me that no one should take treasure from a lady unless he gives a gift in return."

At that there was a roar of laughter. The little strutting knight laughed loudest of all.

"Who are you that you make so merry because I would defend the queen?" Percival demanded of him.

"I am Sir Kay, the king's steward, and I keep watch over this castle," the knight said. "I need no help from a country waif."

At that moment there slipped past Sir Kay's elbow a dwarf. This dwarf was hardly older than Percival himself. He had been at court only a year, and during that time he had neither smiled nor spoken a word, since he was lonely for his faraway parents and his brothers and sisters.

Looking up at the tall lad on the low pony, the dwarf thought that this was the kindest face he had seen since he had left his home.

"Greetings to you, young stranger," he said. "May you bring honor to the queen."

"That I will right quickly," replied Percival. But Sir Kay raised his lance and struck the dwarf so hard a blow that he fell to the floor.

"Now I have two wrongs to avenge, tall man," Percival cried, angrily mocking Sir Kay for his short stature. "When I have finished these two tasks, I shall come back to Camelot to be knighted."

Then Percival rode swiftly out of the castle. Beyond the city walls he saw the Red Knight mounted and waiting beneath a giant oak tree.

"Do they send such a raggle-taggle champion as you from Arthur's court?" the Red Knight scoffed, and he charged so suddenly and fiercely that he knocked Percival from the pony's back. In cruel merriment he lifted the visor of his helmet to look down at the fallen boy.

Percival leaped to his feet and quickly threw his small spear. His aim was so strong and true that the spear went through the Red Knight's eye and came out of the back of his head. The Red Knight fell down dead, and Percival took the queen's golden goblet from the dead man's body.

"I shall also have weapons and a horse," Percival told himself. He seized his enemy's sword and lance and shield, but he could not get the armor off, since he did not know how it was buckled on. In his excitement he began dragging the dead man up and down as he had often seen his mother's servant woman drag an unruly goat. The body would not slip free.

After a while Percival, all breathless, looked up to see that an old man stood watching him.

"If you are willing, I will show you how to unbuckle that armor, lad. It is right that you should have it, for it was this Red Knight who killed your father and brothers," the old man said.

When Percival had donned the armor, the old man asked, "Do you know how to handle that sword and lance?"

"I would know well enough if someone would show me," Percival answered.

"Then come with me. I am your uncle whom you have never known. I am ready to be your teacher."

"My mother told me about you. She said that I should trust you," Percival said.

So he spent several months at his uncle's castle, learning the use of sword and lance, learning also the rules of chivalry which every courteous knight must follow.

"Remember above all," the old man admonished him, "do not ask rude questions. Wait for understanding."

When his teacher thought him ready, Percival rode out into the world again. He met and jousted with sixteen knights and defeated every one of them. Those who were strong enough to leave the jousting field he bade go at once to Camelot and tell King Arthur who had vanquished them. But he did not entrust to anyone Queen Guinevere's golden goblet. He carried it with him always.

After many adventures Percival came on a winter's day to a beautiful castle. This time he tethered his horse by the castle moat and walked into the great hall. There he found a table set for chess. When he seated himself and began to move the white chessmen, the red men moved of themselves. Three times they checkmated him. It came to him then that only magic could defeat him in this way, since his mother had taught him to be a skillful and subtle player.

The magic had just begun. Looking up from the chessboard he saw a beautiful lady coming to take her place at his side. The lady had eyes as blue as chicory petals and skin as white as campion flowers. On her finger was a gold ring with a diamond stone. He knew at once that she was Blanchefleur, the lady of the azure tent.

Her presence filled him with such delight that, when an hour had passed, he said to her, "Blanchefleur, you are surely the most beautiful lady in the world. I promise to love you and be faithful to you forever. Will you be my lady wife?"

"I love you dearly, handsome youth," Blanchefleur replied, "but the time has not come for us to be together."

At that moment a miraculous procession came through the

castle hall. First came a maiden in a long white veil who carried before her, also veiled, what seemed to be a cup so dazzling that Percival did not dare look directly at it but instead sank to his knees, half covering his eyes. As he did so, a second lady followed the first. Then came a third who carried a long spear from whose tip fell three drops of blood. As the three vanished, a fragrance as of roses and spices filled the air.

Percival knew that he must ask no questions, but he leaped to his feet, exclaiming silently to himself, "Surely I must follow that veiled cup!"

In that instant the magic visions of the day were ended. The lady Blanchefleur disappeared as though she had been a spirit maiden. The beautiful castle itself, hall and towers and wide moat, vanished also.

Percival found himself alone upon his horse with snow falling white about him. Above his head a hawk and dove were struggling, and the hawk killed the dove so that three drops of her blood fell upon the snow. Percival thought of the veiled cup and the magic spear and strange tales his mother had told him, but he thought also of Blanchefleur.

So deep were these thoughts that he fell into a kind of trance, not seeing what took place around him.

Suddenly he felt a sword blade touch his shoulder and heard a mocking voice from behind a closed visor. "Why do you not speak to me, Red Knight? I am one of King Arthur's company of the Round Table, and I address you in the king's name. We are a royal hunting party and have called to you, yet you sit like one who has lost his senses. Fie upon your discourtesy!"

At that rude challenge Percival drew his sword and attacked the stranger so fiercely that the other soon fell to the ground and went limping away.

Percival was again lost in thought when a second rider reined in his horse beside him. This man had a silver voice.

"Know, sir, that I am Gawain, knight of the Round Table," the man said. "King Arthur and his companions, I among them, have seen you here upon this hill deep in thought. If you are willing, we would speak with you. Yet I see that you must be dreaming of some most serious matter, or of the lady whom you love."

"I dream of both," Percival said, recognizing the voice as that of the courteous knight who had first spoken to him in the wilderness. "I beg you, Sir Gawain, tell me who was that rude fellow who came to me just now?"

"He was Sir Kay," Gawain answered. "Though not tall he is a skillful jouster, but you are young and strong. You broke his shoulder when you flung him from his horse."

Then Percival cried, "Now I have avenged the two wrongs which I vowed to make right. I have killed the Red Knight who dishonored Queen Guinevere, and I have defeated Sir Kay, who struck down the dwarf. I will come with you willingly." He rode with Sir Gawain to where King Arthur sat his mount, and he gave him the queen's golden goblet which he carried with him.

So he was invited to return to Camelot in honor. At Camelot the king knighted him and gave him a place at the Round Table between the seat of Sir Gawain and that mysterious, veiled chair which men spoke of in whispers as the Siege Perilous. He was now Sir Percival of Wales.

With the king's permission, he went back to bring his mother out of the wilderness hiding place to her own long-deserted castle, and in time he proved himself by many more valiant deeds.

Yet always in his heart remained two longings—to find Blanchefleur and to see again the dazzling cup which the veiled maiden had carried in procession, for it seemed to him that it might be the Holy Grail.

SEVEN

Of the Coming of Sir Galahad

With Queen Guinevere at his side and his brave knights gathered round him, Arthur long ruled England justly and wisely.

After the first years of his reign he was no longer a smooth-cheeked boy but a valiant battle leader with a red-gold beard. Men called him *dux bellorum*, war leader. As time passed, lesser kings and lords chose peace and came to Camelot to pledge him their loyalty. Not even the most wicked and ambitious any longer openly challenged his right to wear the crown.

To add to the luster of their good king's name, many of his companions rode out from the royal court to do deeds of valor and to succor those who were in danger or distress. They broke spells of black magic, won freedom for captive knights, and rescued beautiful ladies from dark dungeons and castles of imprisonment. One evil lord boasted that he fringed his mantle with the beards of the men he had killed. Against him the knights of the Round Table jousted so fiercely that his boasting was stilled.

Yet it was true, even in this rich and contented land, that the greatest dream of Arthur's realm had not been realized. No one had looked full upon that heavenly cup, the Holy Grail, whose appearance had been so long promised.

It was also true that amid the one hundred and fifty seats about the Round Table there still stood one seat which had never through the years been used. No one, not even the king himself, had ever dared to tear aside the veil which hung upon that Siege Perilous, Seat of Danger.

All could see that the veil was of richest silk shot through with silver threads, and all guessed that beneath the silk a name would be written in letters of gold upon the ebony wood. But no one could guess whose name that was.

There were some who thought that Sir Lancelot, as Arthur's dearest friend and chief knight of the realm, should leave his own seat and claim the magic chair. But Lancelot knew well that, although he had won great fame and the good king's trust, his own heart was not fully filled with the love of God. It was Queen Guinevere who was enthroned there. He knew, too, that death awaited any proud and self-seeking man who tried the Seat of Danger.

So matters stood one bright spring morning when all the knights were gathered together at Camelot to celebrate once again the Feast of Pentecost. This feast remained very dear to Arthur because it was at Pentecost that his knights renewed their vows each year. Besides, the king was never so happy as when his knights were returned from their adventures and gathered around him.

He sat in his high seat, Sir Lancelot at his left hand, and, well content, he looked around the banquet hall. It seemed to him that this Pentecost would not be like others which had gone before it. Today's feast would be a feast of miracles.

Already on this day the people of Camelot had heard marvelous stories.

Of a jeweled sword set deep in a cube of red marble that had suddenly appeared by the edge of the river flowing through the royal city.

Of a tall young boy pledged secretly to knighthood who would come soon to claim the Seat of Danger.

Of the Holy Grail returned after long years to earth.

That last was the most marvelous story of all.

Long ago a worthy man named Joseph of Arimathea had carried the Grail out of Palestine to bring it to safety in the famed city of Sarras. The people of Sarras had grown so wicked, however, that they could not see the holy cup, and it was secretly carried away from them, also—no one knew how or where. Men remembered only the prophecy that one day the Grail would be seen again by the purest knight on earth.

King Arthur thought of these many things as he sat at the Pentecostal feast table, and his thoughts were very deep.

Suddenly there was a stirring at the far end of the hall. The door there slowly opened to reveal two strangers.

One of the two was a bearded hermit. The other was a tall and handsome youth in crimson armor, a cloak of ermine flung about his shoulders.

Most astonishing, in this warriors' hall whose walls were ablaze with shields and spears, neither stranger carried a weapon of any kind. The youth did wear a scabbard, but it hung empty at his side.

Sir Kay, always short of temper, rose fiercely from his seat. "Who has invited you to the king's banquet hall?" he demanded of the strangers.

The two stood fearless. It was as though Sir Kay's words were carried away from them upon the breeze—although there was no breeze, for now the castle door was closed by unseen hands and every knight sat still.

"My lords, peace to you," the hermit said to the company. And to King Arthur he said, "Sire, I bring to you this young knight of noble blood who will one day achieve the greatest adventure ever attempted in all your realm."

Arthur courteously replied, "You are welcome, worthy hermit. The young knight is welcome, also."

But some in that great hall looked closely at the handsome youth, and they saw that in hair, eyes, and stature, in dignity too, he was remarkably like Sir Lancelot. Abruptly Sir Lancelot himself rose from his seat at the king's side, a strange glow upon his cheeks.

"Sire," he said, "I must tell you and all this company that the youth who comes here today is no chance stranger, but my son, Galahad. For eighteen years he has lived hidden, guarded by nuns who cherished him and taught him those things which a pure soul should know. Now he must gain still other knowledge if he is to come to his full stature. Only yesterday I secretly knighted him at a chapel in the forest. I beg you, greet him kindly."

Arthur reached out a welcoming hand, and the young man bowed. Then without a sign of fright or unease he stepped toward the Round Table and the Seat of Danger. Very calmly he lifted up the silken veil so that everyone in the hall could see the name written there in letters of gold: SIR GALAHAD. And Sir Galahad sat upon the Seat of Danger as though he had been expecting this moment all his life.

When Arthur and the others had recovered a little from their amazement, they led Galahad to the block of red marble floating at the river's edge and pointed out to him the jeweled sword sunk deep into the stone. Since its appearance, many knights had tried to draw out that sword, but not even the strongest had been able to move it. Now they saw, newly appeared upon the marble, letters written in bright gold which read: THIS SWORD IS FOR THE NOBLEST KNIGHT IN THE WORLD WHO WILL SEE WITH HIS OWN EYES THE HOLY GRAIL.

Sir Galahad, though he had lived among the gentle nuns and knew nothing of battle, gravely closed his hand about the hilt of that sword. He drew very strongly and smoothly. The steel blade slipped up from the stone as easily as a bird's wing mounts the air, and Sir Galahad put it into his empty scabbard.

After that another and yet greater miracle took place. When the knights had returned to their seats at the Round Table, the door and windows of the great hall closed, although untouched by human hands. But there was no darkness. Light seven times brighter than the light of the sun dazzled every eye. Perfume like that of the sweetest springtime wafted through the air. On every knight's plate appeared the food which he liked best, ripe fruits, rich meats, and sweet cakes. It seemed a kind of heavenly nourishment, not like any ever carried from the castle kitchen.

Suddenly, amid these wonders, all eyes lifted, for from the vault of the ceiling a glowing cup descended, its outline glimmering beneath a heavy velvet veil.

No one could measure how long the vision lasted. It may have been no more than the indrawing of a breath.

Then unseen hands lifted up the cup, still covered by the velvet veil, so that it rose high and vanished. Everything in the hall looked as it had looked before. Yet everything was changed.

"It is a vision of the Holy Grail which has appeared to us," King Arthur said. "That sacred cup has been hidden for long years, though the best of men have prayed to look upon it. Even today no one of us has seen more than the veiled outline. But all this is a sign. The time has come when a young and unstained knight will look full upon the Grail and win undying glory for himself and all this court.

"So now let every knight who loves God and the king vow to search for the Grail through all the world until it has been found."

At the good king's words every knight at the Round Table lifted up his sword as though he held a cross and took the holy vow.

Yet when the vow had been spoken, King Arthur bowed his

head, and Queen Guinevere, who had come into the hall at word of the miraculous vision, could not hide her tears. They both knew that because of this great quest, the seats about the Round Table would be empty for a long time. It might even be that some of those seats would never again be filled, since many knights might die in perilous adventure before they could return to Camelot.

Queen Guinevere whispered, "Sire, how can you bid them go?"

But Arthur answered, "It must be so, lady."

For his part, the young Sir Galahad had no such sad thoughts. He was not yet certain of what he was to accomplish and only half guessed that all those magic sayings spoke of him, but he was not afraid to ride out alone into the world.

As he took the road which led from Camelot, he saw a young girl upon a white horse leading a jet-black stallion.

"The stallion is for you, Sir Galahad," she said. "I see that you already have a jeweled sword, but you have no shield. Follow me and I will lead you to a shield of magic which will forever keep you safe from harm."

Very readily Sir Galahad mounted the black stallion and followed the girl across the plain.

At dusk they came to a lonely monastery. There the maiden vanished, but as Sir Galahad knelt in prayer, he saw upon the chapel wall a snow-white shield marked with a cross the color of new-shed blood.

It is a most beautiful shield, he thought, but I must not touch it until God wills.

At supper that night he found that he was not the only one

of King Arthur's knights who had found his way to this place. Beside him at table sat the grizzled knight Sir Bagdemagus.

"It is well for you, youth, that you have not touched the shield in the chapel," said Sir Bagdemagus. "I have fought many battles, and tomorrow I will take that shield and go out to seek more adventures with it. The monks here say that it must belong only to the greatest and purest of all knights, and it will bring disaster to any other man who carries it. All the same, I shall try my fortune."

Galahad stayed in the monastery the next day in prayer. At evening he saw Sir Bagdemagus returning on foot, staggering so that he could hardly stand. Blood flowed like a terrible red robe down his face and body.

Galahad rushed to his side. "What has happened to you, sir?" he cried.

"I rode out this morning with the chapel shield," Sir Bagdemagus groaned. "In a valley nearby I was attacked by one who called himself the White Knight. He rode a stallion so tall that my own mount was a pony beside him. I never met a jouster of such strength. He flung me from my horse and chopped and hewed at me so mercilessly that I thought he would surely kill me. Even now I am not certain that the good monks will be able to save my life.

"Alas, I see too late that the saying is true. Only the purest knight of all the realm should dare to touch this shield. Take it. I believe it is yours, Sir Galahad."

The next day Galahad, having said his prayers, rode out upon his black stallion, armed with the jeweled sword and the white shield with the blood-red cross. In the valley he met the mysterious White Knight and saluted him fearlessly.

That fierce man humbly bowed his head. "I have awaited you a long time, Galahad," he said. "Today my waiting is at an end. I am content. Ride on your holy quest with my blessing."

And now Sir Galahad was fully armed and ready to protect himself against any attack which he might meet upon his way. But he hoped he would be able to accomplish his great mission in peace. He did not want to kill any man.

EIGHT

Of the Quest for the holy Grail

On a day some time after Galahad had ridden out from the monastery, he saw in a wood a forbidding castle. Pitiful cries sounded from its grim and storm-dark towers.

Beside the castle drawbridge crouched a crippled graybeard.

"You would do well to turn away from this place, bold youth," the graybeard warned.

"I think you do not know me, good old man," Sir Galahad replied. "I am Galahad, the son of Sir Lancelot, and I come from Arthur's court. I hear pitiful cries which tell me that there are prisoners within this castle. Tell me how I can help them."

"Do not try that." The old man sighed. "You have not the years or strength to defeat the masters of this evil place."

At that moment the castle drawbridge was flung down and ten knights in sable armor galloped across it. Without word or warning the knight who rode first attacked Galahad as if he meant to kill him instantly.

The marvel was that the sable knight's ashwood spear slipped from Galahad's magic shield as easily as a leaf drops from an autumn bough.

Filled with the knowledge of his own power, Sir Galahad for the first time drew his sword. He struck his attacker with such violence that the wicked knight's neck was swiftly broken. With a great moan the man dropped dead upon the ground.

Seeing their leader slain, the nine other knights charged forward, but Sir Galahad struck so fiercely and so skillfully, right and left, that soon two more of those knights lay dead. Three fell into the moat and four fled into the forest.

Then a host of captive knights and ladies, too many to be counted, poured joyously out from the castle and hailed Sir Galahad as their deliverer. But when the bishop of that region came to welcome the young champion, Sir Galahad sadly bowed his head. "I would not have killed these knights if they had not first tried to kill me," he said.

"Do not mourn," answered the bishop. "This was as worthy a deed as has ever been done in this place, for these were wicked men. Though you are young and untried, with the help of God and your own pure heart you have conquered ten."

"Come! Join us in a feast in your honor, Sir Galahad," the rejoicing people cried.

But Galahad blushed in answer. "I thank you, kind knights and ladies, yet I cannot stay for feasting. My time is short, and I must find the Holy Grail."

So he rode on alone, until after some days he found himself at the door of a forest chapel which he had never seen before. On the threshold lay an ancient man with flowing white hair and beard. Galahad spoke to him gently. "I am a knight of King Arthur's Round Table."

"Hear my story, noble knight." The old man groaned. "Once I was king of the famed city of Sarras where the Holy Grail was last seen on earth. But I grew proud and greedy. I dared to kneel at the high altar of Sarras cathedral and to look full upon the Grail. Because I was unworthy, I was made blind.

"I have lain sightless in this deserted place for three hundred years. I cannot die in peace until a knight comes to me who shall in God's good time find the Grail."

"I am that one," Galahad said. For now he was certain of his destiny. He took the blind king into his arms, and the old man looked with clear eyes full into the young knight's face and so he died contented.

Again Sir Galahad rode on.

He met with many adventures and did many deeds of mercy. He healed men wounded almost unto death. He forgave some who had dishonored themselves. He won back ancient rights for a countryside long ruled by tyrants.

And there came a day, upon a lonely shore, when he met with his own father, Sir Lancelot. At first the two did not recognize each other and jousted playfully until Sir Lancelot exclaimed, "Now truly in all the world the only young knight who jousts so well is my son, Galahad." Then they raised their visors and greeted each other with great delight.

Six months they spent upon that shore and on a ship at sea, always rejoicing in each other's company. It was the only time in their lives that they were to spend together.

But Galahad knew that he must not linger longer.

"I must go on my way," he said. "I have a mission to perform." And so they sadly parted.

At last, on a warm evening when summer fruits hung heavy on the trees, Galahad found himself on a deserted plain which was entirely strange to him. There, as he was making a supper of ripe apricots, a maiden appeared. Her dark hair was bound with a silver ribbon, and her voice was like the music of falling waters.

"I beg you, come with me, Sir Galahad," she said. "I promise to lead you to an adventure unlike any other you have known."

Willingly Galahad took up his sword and shield, mounted his jet-black stallion, and followed his guide away across the plain. All around them was the stillness of the nighttime, and overhead and around them lay the white sheen of the moon.

They rode until by and by they reached a promontory which rose at the edge of the plain. Looking down from that height, Galahad saw the sea and a small boat swaying beside a wave-swept rock. Under the linen awning of that boat he saw two knights whom he knew to be from Arthur's court, Sir Percival and Sir Bors.

At once Sir Percival and Sir Bors called out a greeting. "Join us!"

Sir Galahad thought that he could not have truer companions. Sir Bors was cousin to Sir Lancelot. He was a good and simple knight who had so great a longing to find the Grail that he had vowed to sleep upon stone floors and live upon bread and water until he had accomplished his quest. Sir Percival, though he had come to Arthur's court an awkward wilderness boy, had since that time done many valiant deeds and won true knighthood.

Before Galahad could thank his guide for bringing him to such company, she had vanished. So he leaped from his stallion, went down the cliff, and stepped into the waiting boat. The boat with the three knights aboard it drifted from the promontory and out upon the sea.

Surely the waves will soon destroy this small vessel, Galahad thought, but he was not afraid.

At dawn a splendid ship with silken sails and blue-and-scarlet prow appeared on the horizon.

"See how quickly it bears down upon us!" Sir Percival cried.

The ship did indeed approach swiftly, although no sailors or any other human beings were to be seen upon the decks. As the prows touched, Sir Galahad, Sir Percival, and Sir Bors left their own small boat and boarded the miraculous new ship.

Wordless with wonder, they searched through it until in an inner cabin they came upon a table of silver, very finely wrought. A veil of purple velvet was hung across the table, and beneath it shone a dazzling light. Sweet perfume wafted through the air.

It seemed to Sir Galahad that he was at last near the end of his quest, but even now he dared not lift the velvet veil.

All that day he sailed with his companions. At evening he saw a curving shore and, rising beyond it, a beautiful city, its towers and steeples gilded by the setting sun. He heard a voice saying, "Behold, Galahad! This is the far-famed city of Sarras, the city where you will look upon the Grail."

To his wondering companions, Sir Galahad said, "See, there in the midst of Sarras rises a great cathedral. Surely that is where the silver table belongs. We must take it there."

But the table with the velvet veil and the glowing wonder

upon it proved to be the heaviest weight that any man had ever lifted. The three knights staggered beneath the burden and would surely have fallen, except that at the city gates Sir Galahad saw a cripple squatting upon the ground.

"Alms, noble sirs," the cripple wailed. "Give me alms. I have not walked without a crutch for full ten years. I cannot earn my bread."

Sir Galahad very lovingly took the man's hand and touched it to the silver table, and the man stood straight and tall.

Together the four carried the table to the cathedral and placed it upon the high altar.

When news of the miracle spread through the city, the people cried out, "Let the good young knight Sir Galahad be named our king, for we are much in need of him."

Now the ruler of Sarras at that time was a jealous tyrant who would not give up his power. He dared not kill Sir Galahad, Sir Percival, and Sir Bors outright, but he threw them into a deep dungeon. There he kept them in chains for a full year until he himself fell mortally ill. As he lay dying, he granted the prisoners their liberty and begged their forgiveness for the evil he had done them. They granted it to him freely.

So at last, on a sunlit day with the springtime world bright about him, Sir Galahad knew that his great time had come. With Sir Percival and Sir Bors he went again to the cathedral. On the high altar he found the silver table with the velvet veil.

Without fear or pause Sir Galahad lifted up the veil so that he saw with his own eyes the full glory of the Holy Grail. His companions hid their eyes.

As Galahad fell to his knees, a voice sounded.

"Greetings, hero. Praise be to you. You have found the holy cup which once vanished from this place and which now is to be lifted up from earth to heaven where it will stay forever."

As the voice died away, two hands, like doves, very white and shining, appeared in the glowing air. They took the Grail and lifted it high, high, up through the very roof of the cathedral until it could be seen no more. With its going the cathedral organ pealed out a triumphant anthem, such as had never been heard from any earthly instrument.

Sir Galahad cried out in joy, "Thanks be to God that I have accomplished my life's mission. Now may I be granted my final prayer. I beg to be lifted up into heaven. There is no wonder left for me on earth."

Then Galahad turned to Sir Bors. "Ride back to Camelot, kinsman," he said. "Tell my father, Lancelot, what I have seen today. Tell him that, though I go from him, I love him well."

As he spoke, the cathedral organ thundered a yet more marvelous anthem of triumph and thanksgiving.

Sir Percival and Sir Bors uncovered their faces and looked at their companion. They saw that Galahad's soul was being lifted up into heaven by angel hands. His body was dead.

There were both mourning and rejoicing in the city of Sarras on that day and for many days to come. When the mourning time was ended, the people gathered together and chose Sir Percival as their new king. Blanchefleur, the Lady of the White Flower, whom he had long loved, was brought over land and sea to be his bride. The two promised to rule with courtesy and justice so that the city of Sarras was well pleased.

As for Sir Bors, he rode back to Camelot to tell the glorious story.

The knights of the Round Table who had vainly sought the Grail and returned to Camelot unsatisfied—all these and King Arthur too—gave thanks that the purest and noblest of their company had won the surpassing honor.

Arthur himself remembered that Merlin the Magician had prophesied that all this would come to pass. Merlin had also prophesied that later there would come a dark and terrible time when the last great battle of the West would be fought. In that battle the knights of the Round Table would turn upon one another. Some among them would even turn upon their king, and Camelot would be destroyed.

But on this day Arthur chose not to think of that grim warning. Instead, he joined his companions in heartfelt rejoicing that Sir Galahad had found the Holy Grail.

NINE

Of the Last Battle

After the death of Galahad, when the Holy Grail had disappeared from earth, the great quest ended. And of those knights who returned to Arthur's court after fruitless wanderings, some began to ask among themselves who was true to the king, and who was false, through coldness of heart or ambition for the throne. The knights of the Round Table no longer fought for the glory of the court and the common good of all, for they saw that King Arthur's strength was failing. His beard was white, and Merlin no longer stood at his side.

Merlin had grown very old, and with an old man's folly he had fallen in love with Vivien, the Lady of the Lake. He followed her night and day, begging for her love, until she grew weary of him. She asked him to tell her a spell for sleeping, and when he gave her the secret, she put him to sleep and imprisoned him with another spell. She stole his magic book, which was lost forever.

It may be that Merlin's prison is a house of glass, or a bush of whitethorn laden with bloom. Perhaps he sleeps surrounded by perpetual mist on some mountain of Wales, or as the ancient books say, he may rest in "a close neither of iron nor steel nor timber nor of stone, but of air without any other thing, by enchantment so strong that it may never be undone while the world endures." No man knows where Merlin sleeps. As the magician had foreseen, Arthur missed him sorely when trouble came to the Round Table.

The worst trouble came through the best of King Arthur's knights.

Sir Gawain and Sir Lancelot were noble friends, dear to the king and dear to each other, but Sir Gawain became jealous of Sir Lancelot, and a bitter quarrel arose between them. Lancelot was fiercely proud and hot-tempered in battle, and in the fighting he killed two brothers of Gawain. Sir Gawain was sorely grieved by the deaths of his brothers, and told the king that Lancelot was a traitor, so that Arthur banished Lancelot from the court. Sir Lancelot would not fight against his liege lord, King Arthur, but withdrew across the sea to his old castle in France.

When Lancelot had gone, Sir Gawain said to the king, "Follow him, Sire, and attack him!"

But King Arthur said, "Many a time he has rescued you and me, both on horseback and on foot."

"No," Sir Gawain answered, "all that is over now. He is false to you and me." At last he persuaded the king.

Arthur was full of years and his heart was heavy with care, but he made a great host ready. Then he called his nephew Sir Mordred, half brother to Sir Gawain, to be chief ruler of all

England. And Mordred was very pleased, since he had long plotted to gain the throne.

Then King Arthur and Sir Gawain departed from England with their army. It was a multitude that sailed across the narrow sea from Dover and landed with the king on the coast of France. They rode over hill and valley with armor shining and with banners streaming in the wind, until they came to a plain where stood the castle of Sir Lancelot.

Within his castle walls, Sir Lancelot heard the distant thunder of trampling war-horses. Hastening to the battlements, he looked out and saw the army coming in a cloud of dust. Riding in the forefront was his once-loved friend Sir Gawain at the side of King Arthur. And the army advanced until it stood at the very foot of the castle walls and encamped there, besieging the castle.

Then Lancelot said, "Peace is better than war. I shall send a messenger to my lord Arthur to ask for a treaty."

Arthur would have granted the treaty, but Sir Gawain would not, and Arthur heeded the words of Gawain.

So there was much cruel and bitter fighting, and many on both sides lost their lives. Sir Lancelot could not himself fight willingly against his old companions of the Round Table, but remained within the castle and sent others out to fight in his stead.

Sir Gawain, bent on avenging the deaths of his brothers, rode every day on his great war-horse up and down in front of the gates, shouting insults and taunting Lancelot for his want of courage and honor, until Sir Lancelot knew that a battle against his friend must come. On a fateful day the drawbridge fell, and he rode out to face Sir Gawain.

Three times these gallant knights charged fiercely against each other and neither could gain the victory. Then with a mighty thrust Sir Lancelot's sword sheared through the armor of Sir Gawain and through his shoulder and his chest, and Sir Gawain fell to the ground. Sir Lancelot rode back to his castle very sorrowfully, and the gates closed behind him.

Sir Gawain lay sick near a month. Before his wounds could heal, there came from England evil tidings that Mordred had seized both the throne and crown of Britain, telling the people that Arthur had been killed. When Arthur heard this, he withdrew his army from France and returned in haste to England with his great fleet of ships and galleys.

As they came close to the cliffs of Dover, they saw Mordred with his army drawn up to meet them. Then there was a beaching of great boats and small and much slaughter of knights and noble men. But King Arthur leaped into the shallow water and fought his way to land so bravely that no man might prevent him, and his knights fiercely followed him, until Sir Mordred fled with all his people.

When this battle was done, Sir Gawain was found in a boat, lying half dead. And the king, kneeling down, took Sir Gawain in his arms. "Alas," he said, "in Lancelot and you I had my greatest joy. Now must I lose you both?"

"My death day is come," said Gawain, "and all through my own folly. I am struck in the old wound which Lancelot gave me. Had he been with you as he once was, this unhappy war had never begun, for his strength held your enemies at bay. Give me paper, pen, and ink, and I will beg him to return." Then he wrote to Sir Lancelot, "This day I was hurt to the death in the same wound that you gave me. Now for all the love that ever was between us, come over the sea in all haste and rescue the noble king that made you a knight, for Sir Mordred has betrayed him." And Sir Gawain yielded up the spirit.

"I cannot wait for Lancelot," said Arthur. Then he pursued Sir Mordred to the west and they fought again, and the army of King Arthur was victorious, though many noble knights were slain. Again Mordred withdrew, and again he assembled his army, and King Arthur pursued him.

As the king lay asleep in his tent on the battlefield at night, he dreamed a dream, and he saw Sir Gawain, who was dead. Sir Gawain said to the king in his dream, "Sire, God has given me leave to warn you, for if you fight tomorrow with Sir Mordred, you will be slain and your army with you. Do not fight Mordred, but make a treaty until Sir Lancelot and all his noble knights shall come to rescue you with honor." Then the figure of Sir Gawain disappeared.

The king called his knights around him and told them of his vision, and they agreed to make a treaty with Mordred.

Then King Arthur and Sir Mordred vowed to meet in a certain field between the two armies. The place was in a valley near a lake that opened on the western sea. And the two armies were drawn up, facing each other.

King Arthur chose six knights to come with him. Sir Mordred also chose six knights, and it was agreed that none should draw a sword. So when Arthur and Mordred came to sign the treaty, wine was fetched, and they drank together. But it chanced that a snake lay under a bush nearby, and the snake uncoiled itself and slid through the dust and raised its head to strike. One of the knights of Sir Mordred saw the snake and drew his sword to kill it. And when the armies saw that sword drawn, they blew trumpets and shouted grimly, rushing to battle with a sound like thunder. So began the last great battle of the West.

They fought all the day long till it was near night and a hundred thousand lay dead upon the field. In the fall of darkness the king looked about him and cried out in grief, for of all his favorite knights, only one, Sir Bedivere, remained alive, and he was sore wounded. "Now," said Arthur, "I am come to my end and all my court of knighthood with me. Would to God that I could find the traitor."

Then he saw Mordred standing alone, leaning upon his sword among the slain.

"Give me my spear," said Arthur. "There is the man who has worked all this woe."

Sir Bedivere answered, "Sire, let him be. Come what may, he is doomed. If you live, that will be your revenge. Remember your dream and what the spirit of Sir Gawain told you. This unlucky day is past. Let well enough alone."

But the king said, "I shall never have a better chance to kill him. Come life, come death, he shall not escape me." Then he took his spear in both hands and ran toward Sir Mordred, crying, "Traitor, defend yourself."

Mordred heard the king and ran forward with his sword in

his hand. Then King Arthur leveled the spear and drove it with great strength through the body of his enemy. Sir Mordred did not fall but still advanced, thrusting his body forward until the spear stood out an arm's length behind him. Still he came on with his sword held in both hands, smiting Arthur on the side of the head so that he pierced deep through the king's helmet. Then Sir Mordred fell dead to the earth.

Arthur too fell to the earth, fainting. Sir Bedivere lifted him and the king said, "Sir, this is my death wound. Take me from this place."

Sir Bedivere saw a ruined chapel with a broken cross upon the field of battle, not far from the waterside. There he led the king with weak and painful steps. Now while Arthur lay in the chapel, Sir Bedivere heard the sound of people shouting on the field, and from the doorway he saw by the moonlight that robbers were pillaging and looting, taking rings and jewels from the bodies of many noble knights and killing the wounded for their riches. When Sir Bedivere saw it, he would have taken the king to some town for safety, but King Arthur said, "I cannot stand. My time has come. Therefore, take Excalibur, my good sword. Go with it to the lake and throw it into the water. Come quickly back and tell me what you have seen."

Sir Bedivere took the sword and left the chapel. Then, in the moonlight, the golden hilt studded with jewels flashed and blazed in his hand, and he said to himself, "If I throw away this rich sword, no good will come of it, but only loss." And he hid Excalibur under a tree. Then he came again to the king and said that he had thrown the sword into the water.

The king said, "What did you see?"

"Sire," he answered, "I saw nothing but waves and winds."

"You did not obey me," said Arthur. "Go and do my command, if you love me. Throw away the sword."

Sir Bedivere went again, and again when he looked at Excalibur, he thought it sin and shame to throw away that noble sword. So he returned and told the king that he had done his command.

"What did you see?" said the king.

"Sire," he answered, "I saw nothing but the waves breaking on the shore. The tide is going out."

Then Arthur cried, "You have betrayed me twice. You are untrue. Go quickly and obey me, for your long delay puts me in danger of my life. Who would believe that you, whom I made a knight, would see me dead for the sake of a jeweled sword?"

Then Sir Bedivere ran from the chapel to the tree where he had hidden the sword. Swiftly he took it up and went to the lakeshore. There he bound the belt about the hilt and threw the sword as far as he might into the water. Then from the lake there rose a hand and an arm clothed in glittering white that caught the sword and brandished it three times. And the hand and the sword vanished beneath the waves, for it was here that the Lady of the Lake had given the sword to King Arthur.

Sir Bedivere came to the king and told him what he had seen. King Arthur then said, "Help me to the shore."

Sir Bedivere carried the king from the chapel to the edge of the lake. And there, drawn up on the beach he saw a little boat with three fair queens from the Other World standing in it, robed in black. "Now put me into the boat," said the king, and so Bedivere did softly. The queens took King Arthur in their arms and laid him on a couch that was there, weeping all the while.

Then Sir Bedivere cried out, "Ah, my lord Arthur, what shall I say of you to Lancelot when he comes, for he loves you well, and what shall become of your people, left among our enemies without you?"

"Take comfort," said the king. "Fear nothing. Trust in yourselves and do the best that you may. I will go to the vale of Avalon to heal me of my grievous wound. If you never hear of me again, pray for my soul."

Then the boat moved out from the shore, and Sir Bedivere lost sight of it in the darkness.

When Sir Lancelot in France read Gawain's letter telling how Mordred had betrayed the king, he sailed at once for England, bringing with him an army to go to the aid of King Arthur. But it was too late. Gawain lay buried at Dover, the throne was in the hands of Arthur's enemies, and Queen Guinevere had taken refuge in a nunnery. Arthur was gone. Some said he was alive in Avalon, but others said that the three queens had taken his dead body to Glastonbury for burial.

Lancelot left his army encamped at Dover. He told his knights that if he had not returned within two weeks, they should sail for France. Then he rode off westward alone.

A week later he came to a nunnery at Almesbury and stopped to ask for news of the queen. Then one of the nuns, dressed in a black robe and a white veil, fell fainting when she saw him in the cloister. When she came to herself, she said, "Call that knight to me, for I would have a word with him."

And when he was brought to her, she spoke to him before all the nuns. "Through you and me and the false tales men told of us came the end of Arthur's kingdom and the death of my noble lord. I should have sent you from my side long years ago. Therefore, Sir Lancelot, never look upon my face again. Pray for me. But go back to your own castle. Take a wife and live happily with her."

"No, sweet madam," said Sir Lancelot. "That I will never do. I vowed to be true to the king, and I have promised to be true to you as long as I live. I will keep my promise. As you have forsaken the world, so will I. Only kiss me in farewell."

"No," said the queen, "that I must not do."

So they parted. Sir Lancelot rode all day and all night in grief until he came to a hermitage and a chapel between two cliffs at Glastonbury. The hermit there showed him a fresh grave where men had begun to say Arthur's body lay. There Lancelot put on the habit of a monk and served God with prayers and fasting for the rest of his days. At last, word was brought to him that the queen had died. Lancelot brought her body to Glastonbury and laid her in a grave beside the tomb where these words were written: HERE LIES ARTHUR, THE ONCE AND FUTURE KING.

Within a few weeks, Lancelot too died. He was carried to his castle at Joyous Gard, and those who loved him mourned for him, saying, "Ah, Lancelot, you were the best of all worldly knights. You were the most courteous knight who ever carried a shield, the truest friend that ever rode a horse, the truest lover that ever loved a woman. You were the kindest man that ever struck with a sword, the most admirable that ever came among a company of knights, the gentlest to ladies, the sternest knight whenever you leveled your spear against a mortal foe."

As for Arthur, many believe that the grave at Glastonbury does not, after all, hold the king's body but that his wounds were healed in the isle of Avalon, far in the western sea, where it is always summer. In Avalon, they say, the heroes live forever, and those who love Arthur wait until he comes again with all his knights around him.